Stowaway

by Elizabeth Carter

illustrated by Ashleigh Hancock

Harcourt

Orlando   Boston   Dallas   Chicago   San Diego

Visit *The Learning Site!*

www.harcourtschool.com

Life was very difficult for the Albright family in 1892. Despite all their efforts, their farm in Ireland wasn't very productive. It had been a very cold winter, and the previous summer brought very little rain. One afternoon, ten-year-old William was helping his parents pick some vegetables. Judging from the appearance of the fields, the Albrights would have hardly enough food to last the rest of the week.

"William," said his father, "why don't you and Mattie go down to the lake and see if you can catch a fish or two to go with these vegetables?"

"Yes, Dad," said William. His parents watched as William and the dog strolled down toward the lake. A stranger watching them would have thought they didn't have a care in the world—a boy and his dog off to go fishing. But a stranger wouldn't have known how important it was for the boy to catch something. His parents knew only too well.

As soon as William was out of hearing range, his father took his mother's hand. Looking into her eyes, he said, "Shannon, let's leave this country for a better life. We have taken all we can from this land, and it is time for us to move on. I've saved some of the money we got from selling the farm animals to Mr. O'Carroll. There's enough for all of us to leave this farm and sail to America."

Mrs. Albright turned away, but Mr. Albright continued trying to persuade her. "It would be a better life for us, and I think there would be more opportunities for William. We can barely survive here. We can join the Irish settlement in Boston. The ship leaves in five weeks. What do you think?"

"But what about the farm, Cody? Who's going to take care of it?" Mrs. Albright cried.

"I've made arrangements with your brother. He'll take care of everything for us while we're gone. He may even sell the farm later and join us if all goes well for us in our new home across the vast, open sea," Mr. Albright said.

The Albright family spent the next month getting ready to leave Ireland. They said good-bye to their friends, and made final arrangements for the farm. Five weeks later, early in the morning, the Albrights hurried to Dock 3 with their luggage and Mattie. They waited anxiously on the dock, waiting to board the ship. The Albrights climbed aboard with the other passengers, being careful not to hit their heads on the low beams as they headed to their cabin.

The next few hours were exciting for
William.

Several of his cousins and aunts and
uncles had come to see them off. William
stood on the deck and waved good-bye as the
ship pulled away from the land. Then he
spent some time watching the sailors as they
worked among the rigging and the heavy
beams that held the sails.

After a few hours, William began to get
bored. He wanted something to do. He asked
one of the sailors, "Is there anything I can do
to help you?"

"Do you know how to furl a sail, young fellow?" asked the sailor.

"Well, no, I don't. In fact, I don't even know what that means!"

"It's a bit dangerous. If a storm comes up, we have to roll up and fasten, or furl, the sails to the masts. I was only joking when I asked if you could do it. I'm sure your mother wouldn't want you to do anything dangerous," the sailor explained.

"We might be able to find some easier jobs around here to keep you busy, though. Why don't you coil some of these lines of rope? You can stow them for the time being under the stairs that lead below the deck."

"Thanks!" said William, happy to have something to do.

He coiled the ropes, feeling very useful, almost like a real sailor.

As he started to put the lines under the staircase, he noticed something strange. It looked like a pile of blankets in the shadows, in the far corner under the stairs. He thought he saw them moving!

He decided to move the blankets and find out where they belonged. Besides, he needed the space for the lines.

He picked up a couple of the blankets. There, huddled inside, was a girl. She was about his age, and she looked frightened.

"Who are you? What are you doing here?" William asked.

"Hush!" she cried. "Please do not tell on me, I beg you! I am hiding because I have no money to travel across the ocean, but I long to be in America with my parents."

"How long have you been here, huddled
inside this pile of blankets?" William asked.

"I've been hiding here in the darkness
since late last night. I lurked on the docks
until it looked safe to come on board. I've
been here ever since. No one but you has
noticed me yet."

"Well, you can't stay here for the whole
trip. It's too cold out here. What are you
going to do for food?"

"Maybe you could bring me some," she
said, shyly.

As William talked to the girl, his parents were talking with the ship's captain. They were discussing the wonderful opportunities that America had and the vast, open spaces of land that were there for the taking.

"Well, that's what I've heard, anyway," said Mr. Albright. "And I'll be right there in the front of the line when they're handing out the deeds for the new settlement. Just think of it, Shannon. Won't that be wonderful?"

Mrs. Albright agreed. "I can't wait to set foot on...oh my, William, who is that?" Mrs. Albright cried out in amazement.

William and the girl were approaching the adults.

"This is my new friend. I found her under the staircase," William explained to his parents. Then he turned to the captain and said, "Captain, sir, she says she can work on the ship and help you sail to America. She has no money, but she will help in any way she can. Her family is already in America, and she doesn't want to go back to Ireland," said William.

"Well," said the captain, "stowing away is serious business, but I guess I can't exactly drop you off into the ocean now that we've left the port. I suppose I can find a few jobs for you to do around here to pay for your passage."

"Thank you, sir. I promise that I won't be any trouble," the girl said.

"What's your name, dear?" asked Mrs. Albright. "Where are your folks? Do they know where you are?"

"My name is Colleen, ma'am. My parents have already gone to America. They said they would send for me as soon as they could. I've been staying with my grandmother, but she got sick, so she went to the hospital. While I lurked in a corner, I overheard talk about putting me in an orphanage. But I know my parents want me with them."

"Well," said the captain, "do you have an address for your parents?"

"Yes," said Colleen, showing the captain a scrap of paper from her pocket.

"Ah, Boston, Massachusetts. You're lucky.
That's where we're headed," said the captain.
"We'll contact your parents as soon as we
land. But now, I'm sure you're hungry, and it's
just about time to eat dinner. Let's get you
fed and find you a place to sleep. Tomorrow
we can talk about how you can help around
here."

William and Colleen smiled. Their
unknown future in America didn't seem quite
as scary with a new friend.